# MY BIG BOOK OF FINGER PLAYS

## A Fun-to-Say, Fun-to-Play Collection

by Daphne Hogstrom

illustrated by Sally Augustiny

 **GOLDEN PRESS**

Western Publishing Company, Inc.
Racine, Wisconsin

© 1974 by Western Publishing Company, Inc.
All rights reserved. Produced in U.S.A.

GOLDEN, A GOLDEN BOOK®, and GOLDEN PRESS®
are trademarks of Western Publishing Company, Inc.

Second Printing, 1974

Start with closed fists facing toward you.
Raise thumb of left hand on word ONE.

Keep fingers raised on left hand.
Raise little finger on right hand.

Raise thumb on right hand.

# One, Two, Three

ONE is a cat that says meow.

TWO is a dog that says bowwow.

THREE is a crow that says caw, caw.

FOUR is a donkey that says hee-haw.

FIVE is a lamb that says baa, baa.

SIX is a sheep that says maa, maa.

SEVEN is a chick that says chuck, chuck.

EIGHT is a hen that says cluck, cluck.

NINE is a cow that says moo, moo.

TEN is a rooster crowing COCK-A-DOODLE-DOO!

Now tuck hands under arms and move elbows up and down in motion of flapping wings.

4

# Fingers, Fingers

Fingers, fingers,
Flit and fly.
Fingers, fingers,
Climb up high.
Fingers, fingers,
Turn and twist.
Fingers, fingers,
Make a fist.
Fingers, fingers,
Crawl and creep.
Fingers, fingers,
Fall asleep!

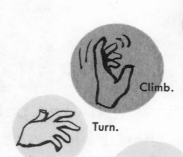

Flutter fingers of both hands.
Flutter in front of you
and then to each side.

Climb.

Turn.

Close hand tightly.

Crawl.

Drop hands limply from wrists.

# Hands

Open them, shut them,
Open them, shut them,
Give a little clap.
Open them, shut them,
Open them, shut them,
Lay them in your lap.
Creep them, creep them,
Creep them, creep them
Slowly to your chin.
Open up your little mouth,
But do not let them in!

5

# My Red Balloon

I had a little red balloon,
But then I blew and blew
Till it became all big and fat
And grew and grew and grew.

I tossed it up into the air
And never let it drop.
I bounced it on the ground, until
It suddenly went POP!

Make small circle.

Blow hard into circle after
each "blew." Continue growth
of circle.

Tossing up motions

Bouncing motions

Hold out hands in surprise.
Clap loudly on "POP!"

6

# Sand Castles

I dug in the sand,
And I carefully made
Five sand castles
With my pail and spade.

I felt like a king (queen)
In a golden crown,
Till the blue sea
Knocked my castles down.

So I dug again
In that sandy shore,
Till I had TEN castles
And was king (queen) once more!

Digging motions

Hold up five fingers.

Stand tall.
Hands form circle over head.

Hold up five fingers. Other
hand makes waves.

Hand making waves closes fingers
of other hand.

Digging motions

Hold up ten fingers.

Stand tall.
Hands form circle over head.

7

# Look! I'm a Dragon!

Look! I'm a dragon!

Look! I'm a mouse!

Look! I'm a castle!

Look! I'm a house!

Look! I'm a mountain!

Look! Here's a well!

Look! Here's a cymbal!

Look! Here's a bell!

Look! I'm a glider!

Look! I'm a car!

Look! Here's a Yo-Yo!

Look! I'm a star!

# I'm a Puppet

Hold out arms and hands loosely.

Move arms and legs as though being pulled by strings.

Wave stiffly.

Throw a kiss jerkily.

Invent motions.

Climbing motions with arms and hands.

Stop motion. Drop limply.

I'm a puppet
On a string.
I can leap,
And I can spring.

I can wave
And throw a kiss.
I can move
My arms like this.

I can even
Climb a wall.
But . . . loose my strings,
And I will fall!

# The Robot

Move arms and legs stiffly, remaining in same place.

Continue walking motions. Add head movement, left and right, then open eyes wide.

Here's a robot,
Big and strong.
Watch him as he
Walks along.

His head turns left,
His head turns right,
And both his eyes
Shine red and bright.

Stop all movement. Press button. Continue head movement, then speak in low voice.

Press this button;
He will say,
"How are all
My friends today?"

Pull this handle;
He will tell:
"I am feeling
Very well!"

Stop all movement. Pull handle. Add head movement, low voice.

# Five Frisky Frogs

Five little frisky frogs
Hopping on the shore:
One hopped into the pond—
    SPLASH!
So then there were just four.

Four little frisky frogs
Climbing up a tree.
One fell into the grass—
    BOOM!
So then there were just three.

Three little frisky frogs
Bathing in the dew.
One caught a sneezy cold—
    AHCHOO!
So then there were just two.

Hold up five fingers.

Hop.

Call *splash* loudly.
Throw hands out and up.

Hold up four fingers.

Climb.

Fall.

Call *boom* loudly.

Hold up three fingers.

Wash face and body.

Cover nose.

Sneeze loudly.

ahchoooo

Hold up two fingers.

Sleep.

Snore loudly.

Hold up one finger.

Lean chin on hand.
Look sad.

Cup hands around mouth.

Hold up five fingers. Smile.

Two little frisky frogs
Sleeping in the sun.
One slept the day away—
    SNORE!
So then there was just one.

One little frisky frog
Sitting on a stone.
Let's call his four friends back—
    YOO-HOO!
So he won't be alone.

# The Small Koala Bear

In faraway Australia,
Across the rolling sea,
There lives the small koala bear,
As cuddly as can be.
He won't eat meat or vegetables.
He won't drink milk or tea.
He just eats eucalyptus leaves
From his eucalyptus tree.

Point with finger.

Make rolling motions.

Hug self.

Put hand to mouth. Head shakes no.

Drink. Head tips back, head shakes no.

Pick and eat. Smile.

14

# Little Squirrel

A little squirrel
Runs and jumps.

Curve hands at chest.
Fingers run.

An eagle
Dives and glides.

One hand dives.
Arms straight out at sides

A monkey swings
From limb to limb—

Swing arms in rhythm.

But a snake
Just slips and slides.

Snaky, slithering motion
with one hand

# The Ringdinkydoo

Here is the captain,
And here is the crew,
Sailing the waves
In the *Ringdinkydoo*.

Salute.

Hold up ten fingers.

Make waves with one hand.

Cup hands around mouth in calling action.

Hands grasp imaginary mop handle.

Mopping motions

"Mop!" calls the captain.
"We'll mop!" cries the crew,
Sailing the waves
In the *Ringdinkydoo*.

"Climb!" calls the captain.
"We'll climb!" cries the crew,
Sailing the waves
In the *Ringdinkydoo*.

Calling action

Climbing motions

"Paint!" calls the captain.
"We'll paint!" cries the crew,
Sailing the waves
In the *Ringdinkydoo*.

Calling action

Painting motions with one hand

16

"Run!" calls the captain.
"We'll run!" cries the crew,
Sailing the waves
In the *Ringdinkydoo*.

For a CAT is the captain,
And MICE are his crew!
Sailing the waves
In the *Ringdinkydoo*.

And he might try to CATCH them
For mousemallow stew!
Sailing the waves
In the *Ringdinkydoo*.

Calling action

Running motions

Make ears.

Cup hands downward
at chest.

Catching movements with hands together
on word CATCH
Rub stomach. Smile.

(This finger play may be continued by the players adding their own
action words, such as *dance, hop,* or *jump,* accompanied by suitable
hand and finger movements. The "run" verse and the two final verses
that follow should be used to complete the finger play.)

17

Thumb and finger form tunnel.
Other hand passes through.

Train hand passes over
upright hand.

Move hand in circles.

Hand pulls whistle cord.

Indicate a row of short cars.

# My Tiny Train

My tiny train
Rolls round and round.
It runs through tunnels
In the ground.
It even climbs
Up mountainsides,
While a whistle blows
As it rides and rides.
WHOO! WHOO! WHOO!

# The Circus Clown

The circus clown
Has a funny face,
With a red, red nose right HERE.
Can YOU make a face
Like a circus clown
With a smile from ear to ear?

Hands indicate cone-shaped hat.

Point to cheeks.

Point to own nose on word HERE.
Point to other child on word YOU.

Point to cheeks.

Draw up sides of mouth with fingers.

# The Mulberry Bush

Here we go round the mulberry bush,
The mulberry bush, the mulberry bush.
Here we go round the mulberry bush,
On a cold and frosty morning.

This is the way we wash our clothes,
We wash our clothes, we wash our clothes.
This is the way we wash our clothes,
On a cold and frosty morning.

This is the way we iron our clothes,
We iron our clothes, we iron our clothes.
This is the way we iron our clothes,
On a cold and frosty morning.

This is the way we sew our clothes,
We sew our clothes, we sew our clothes.
This is the way we sew our clothes,
On a cold and frosty morning.

Twist and twirl fingers in air.

Hug self and shiver.

Up and down sewing motion

Ironing motion

Dipping motion of both hands

# Wee Willie Winkie

Wee Willie Winkie
Runs through the town,
Upstairs and downstairs,
In his nightgown.

Indicate "wee."

Fingers run up . . .
and down.

Reach to the ankles.

Rapping at the window,
Crying through the lock:
"Are the children in their beds?
Now it's eight o'clock!"

Knocking motions

Bend to call through keyhole.

Sleep position

Hold up eight fingers.

21

# Little Red Robins

Little red robins
Flying around,
Up in the treetops,
Down near the ground.

Flutter fingers of both hands.

Flutter fingers before face.

Flutter high.

Flutter low.

Sleep position

Cup hands together.

Continue cupping hands
and look up.

Flutter fingers
out from shoulders.

Drop hands slowly.

Hide hands behind back.

If you are tired,
Here is a nest.
Wouldn't you like
To come down and
rest?

All the red robins
Flutter away,
Saying, "We're sorry,
But we cannot stay."